Aggie and Ben
Three Stories

Lori Ries

Illustrated by **Frank W. Dormer**

ini Charlesbridge

For Tony and Arlene: thank you for sharing your lovable
Aggie. For my wonderful husband: thank you, Dave,
for your constant love and support. And for every child
who has ever loved a dog.
—L. R.

To Mom and Dad, with love
—F. W. D.

2007 First paperback edition
Text copyright © 2006 by Lori Ries
Illustrations copyright © 2006 by Frank W. Dormer
All rights reserved, including the right of reproduction in whole or in part in any form.
Charlesbridge and colophon are registered trademarks of Charlesbridge Publishing, Inc.

Published by Charlesbridge
85 Main Street
Watertown, MA 02472
(617) 926-0329
www.charlesbridge.com

Library of Congress Cataloging-in-Publication Data
Ries, Lori.
    Aggie and Ben / Lori Ries ; illustrated by Frank W. Dormer.
        p. cm.
    Summary: After choosing a new dog, Ben describes what the pet Aggie can do
and should not do around the house.
        ISBN 978-1-57091-594-9 (reinforced for library use)
        ISBN 978-1-57091-649-6 (softcover)
[1. Dogs—Fiction. 2. Pets—Fiction.] I. Dormer, Frank W., ill. II. Title.
PZ7.R429Ag 2006
[E]—dc22   2005028702

Printed in China
(hc) 10 9 8 7 6 5 4 3
(sc) 10 9 8 7 6 5 4 3 2 1

Illustrations done in pen and ink and watercolor on 140-lb. cold-press Winsor and
    Newton paper
Display type set in Tabitha and text type set in Janson
Color separated by Chroma Graphics, Singapore
Printed and bound in China by Everbest Printing Company, Ltd.,
    through Four Color Imports Ltd., Louisville, Kentucky
Production supervision by Brian G. Walker
Designed by Susan Mallory Sherman

The Surprise

"Where are we going?" I ask.
"It's a surprise," Daddy says.

We get into the car.

We go to the pet shop.
That is Daddy's surprise!

I see birds.
"Would you like a bird?" the lady asks.

I think.
A bird would sing.

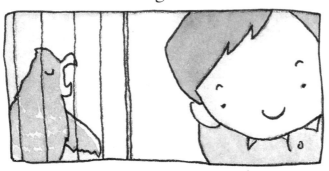

A bird would sit on my finger.

A bird would fly.

But a bird could never play outside. It would fly away.

"I do not think I want a bird," I say.

I see mice.
"Would you like a mouse?" the lady asks.

I think.
A mouse would run through a tube.

A mouse would sit in my hand.

A mouse would hide
in my pocket.

But a mouse might get lost.

"I do not think I want a mouse," I say.

I see snakes.
"Would you like a snake?" the lady asks.

I think.
A snake might be fun.

A snake would wrap around my arm.

A snake would slide across the floor.

But a snake might make Mommy scream.

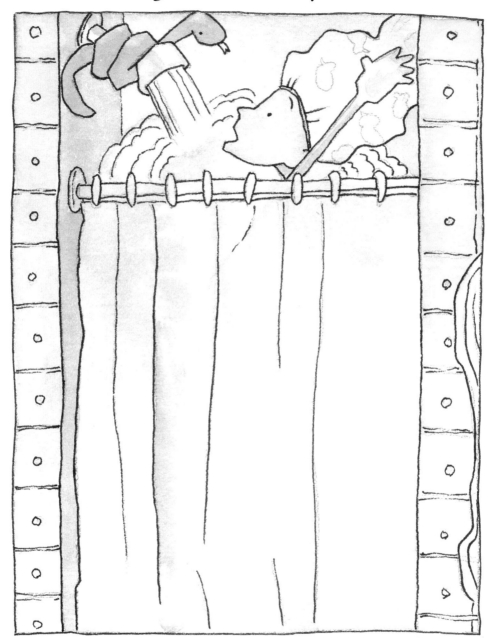

"I do not think I want a snake," I say.

I see cats.
"Would you like a cat?" the lady asks.

I think.
A cat would purr when I pet her.

A cat would chase things.

A cat would play.

But a cat would not play with me at the park.
"I do not think I want a cat," I say.

I see dogs.
"Would you like a dog?" the lady asks.
I think.
A dog would play chase.

A dog would go for walks and play at the park.

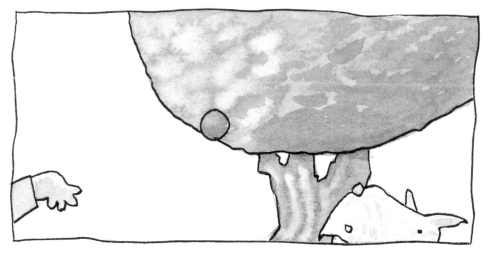

A dog would sleep on my bed and be my best friend!

"I would! I would like a dog!" I say.

We look at the dogs.
One dog makes me laugh.
"Ruff!" she says.

"This one," I say. "I want this one!"
I name her Aggie.

Just Like Aggie

"Look, I'm a dog," I tell Mommy.
"I am just like Aggie!"

Aggie sniffs around her new home.
I sniff around, too.

Aggie sniffs the couch. I sniff the couch, too.
She sniffs the rug. I sniff the rug, too.

Aggie finds Daddy's shoes.
"No, no, Aggie. That is not a toy for you!" I say.

Aggie goes into the kitchen.
She jumps up to the counter.
I jump up to the counter, too.
"Down, Aggie," Mommy says.
"This snack is not for you."

Aggie goes into the laundry room.
I go, too.
She jumps into the dryer.
"No, Aggie," I say. "That is not a bed for you."

Aggie goes into the bathroom.
I go into the bathroom, too.
Aggie sees the toilet.

I am done being a dog.

I get a ball.
"Here is your new toy," I say.
I toss it high. Aggie runs fast!

I get a treat.
"This is a snack for you, Aggie," I say.
Aggie eats it.

I get a bowl.
"This is water for you," I say.
Aggie licks the water. Her ears get wet, too.

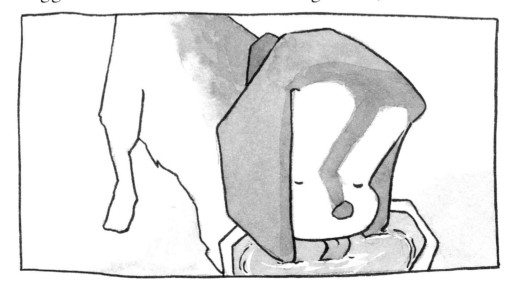

"And you can sleep with me," I tell her.
Aggie is happy. She wags her tail.
Just like Aggie, I am happy, too!

The Scary Thing

"Time for bed," I tell Aggie.
I run up the stairs. Aggie comes, too.

I brush my teeth.
"No, no, Aggie. Toothpaste is not for dogs!" I tell her.

I read Aggie a bedtime story.
"No, no, Aggie," I say. "Do not eat the giant!"

Mommy tucks us in and turns out the light.
My room is dark.

"Ruff!" says Aggie.
I look. Aggie sees something.

Aggie sees something scary on the shelf.

I turn on the light.
"Silly Aggie!" I say. "It is just a truck."

I turn off the light and jump into bed.

"Ruff," Aggie says.
I look. Aggie sees something else.
Something scary is hanging on the wall.

I turn on the light.
"Silly Aggie," I say. "It is just my robe."

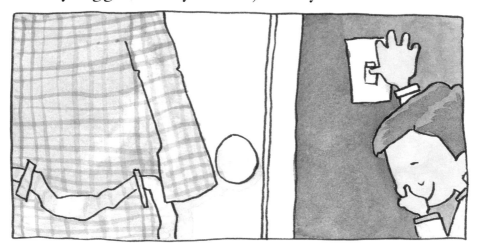

I turn off the light again and jump back into bed.

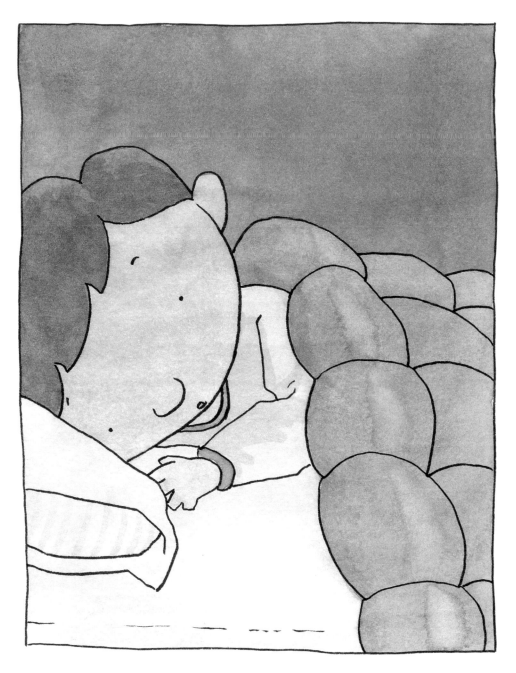

Something scary tugs on the bed.
"Grrrrowl," says Aggie.

"I feel it, too!" I tell her.
I sit up. It tugs again.

I jump out of bed and turn on the light.

"Silly Aggie. You are not so scary now," I say.
I turn off the light and climb into bed.

Aggie lies down to sleep, too.
There is nothing scary.
Just me and Aggie.